Adapted by Beth Beechwood

Based on the series created by Danny Kallis & Jim Geoghan

Based on the episode, "Who's the Boss?," Written by Danny Kallis & Adam Lapidus

New York

Printed in the United States of America

First Edition
1 3 5 7 9 10 8 6 4 2

Library of Congress Catalog Card Number on file.

ISBN 978-1-4231-1942-5

For more Disney Press fun, visit www.disneybooks.com
Visit DisneyChannel.com

Chapter 1

The time had come for Zack Martin to do the unthinkable—he had to get a job. And the most obvious, yet unappealing, option involved none other than his do-gooder identical twin, Cody, and the Paul Revere Mini-Mart. Cody was the store's number one employee, and so he had managed to get Zack a job there as a bag boy.

Since they had moved into the Tipton

Hotel with their mother, Carey, life had been pretty carefree for the twins. But now it was "good-bye" slacking off and "hello" responsibility.

Now Zack found himself on day one of the job in the market he wished he could simply mooch snacks from. And to top it all off, Wayne Wormser, the manager, was about to crown Zack's blond head with a triangular hat in the spirit of Paul Revere himself. This is not cool, Zack thought. It's bad enough I have to wear an apron.

But Wayne was unaware of Zack's musings. "Welcome to the Paul Revere team," he said. "Wear your hat with pride." Wayne beamed as he placed the atrocious hat on Zack's head.

"I'm not sure that's possible," Zack replied flatly. How would he ever live down playing dress-up every day?

"Cody is our senior bag boy," Wayne explained, ignoring Zack's tone. "You can learn a lot from him. Just do whatever he does."

Zack looked at Wayne in disbelief. Was he serious? Do whatever Cody did? That went against everything he believed in. His twin, on the other hand, loved the newfound attention and power he was getting.

"Just do what I do," he repeated smugly.

"You mean moisturize before bed?" Zack retorted.

Cody eyed his brother. "I'll have the last laugh when we're sixty and you look like a prune." He started to march away in a huff before he realized something. "Oh, speaking of which, you know, Wayne, we forgot to put Zack through the initiation ritual."

The manager, who had left the brothers to go and unpack a box near the register, looked up. "Oh, that's right," Wayne remembered as Zack and Cody approached him. "New employees have to drink prune juice mixed with fish oil," he said, pulling a bottle of each out of the box.

"I'm not doing that," Zack said matter-of-factly.

"Okay." Wayne nodded without protest.

Wait, what? Cody thought. "But you made *me* do it," he whined. "You said it was an 'established tradition.'" Cody made quote marks in the air with his fingers for emphasis.

"Yeah, I've been trying to *establish* it for years," Wayne said. "You were the first one stupid enough to do it." He laughed. Being a manager had its perks.

Cody made a face. So far, working with his brother was turning out to be nothing but a major pain.

At least they weren't missing too much back at the hotel. It was a typical day for the Tipton. Which meant, it was *far* from ordinary. Mr. Moseby, the hotel's manager and bane of the twins' existence, was rushing through the lobby when he came upon a large object covered with a green sheet. It wasn't doing anything for the look of the lobby, in his opinion. "Oh, what is this?" Mr. Moseby asked no one in particular.

Suddenly, Arwin, the hotel's maintenance man, popped up from behind the giant eyesore. The lanky man was, as usual, rather disheveled. "Hey, Mr. Moseby!" he cried, causing the manager to scream.

Composing himself, Mr. Moseby gave Arwin a stern look.

"I have a new invention!" Arwin cried,

pointing to the green sheet.

"Oh, dear," Mr. Moseby groaned. When Arwin had a new invention it was rarely something to get excited about. Most often, it was something to *worry* about.

Unfortunately, Arwin didn't notice the fear that had crept into Mr. Moseby's eyes. He was too eager to share. "Ta-da!" Arwin shouted gleefully as he removed the sheet with a flourish. Only, in his attempt at a grand gesture, he threw the sheet off the machine and onto Mr. Moseby, covering him completely.

"Arwin!" Mr. Moseby growled from under the sheet.

Reaching over, Arwin quickly pulled the cloth off his boss. When Mr. Moseby could see, Arwin cried, "Ta-da! Again! It's a letter-sorting machine!" Arwin turned the machine, which looked like an old window air conditioner, toward a set of mail cubbies set up on the hotel's front desk. "It's got a microchip in it that reads each envelope and promptly shoots it into the appropriate cubby."

Mr. Moseby knew where this was going—nowhere good. "Oh, dear," he repeated.

"Ten, nine, eight . . ." Arwin started to count down slowly.

"Arwin!" Mr. Moseby warned.

But instead of stopping, which is what Mr. Moseby wanted, Arwin went full speed ahead. He turned on the machine and letters started flying everywhere. All around them, people began ducking for cover. One letter knocked a man's hat off. Another letter knocked the phone out of the receptionist's hand. All people could do was take cover and hope Arwin knew how to turn the thing off.

But that was too much to hope for. Instead, Arwin simply grabbed a tennis racket from one of the luggage racks a bellboy was pushing through. He started swatting away the letters. "Look, Mr. Moseby, air mail!" he yelled.

Mr. Moseby was *not* amused.

Seeing the unhappy look on the man's face, Arwin's smile faded. "Hit the red button!" he yelled.

Mr. Moseby frantically tried to find the button. He looked to the left, to the right, on the top, and on the bottom. "There is no red button!" he finally yelled.

"Oops," Arwin shrugged. Desperate to put an end to the madness, Mr. Moseby pulled the plug on the mail machine. When the letters finally settled, Arwin sauntered over to the cubbies. He pulled out a letter—the only one that had made it into an opening. He proudly held up the envelope. " 'Mr. Marion Moseby,' " he said, reading the address aloud. "Can I call you Mary?" he asked, smiling.

"Would you stop it?!" Mr. Moseby shouted. He started to storm off. "Oh, will someone please clean up my lobby?" he asked over his shoulder. The day was *not* off to a good start.

Chapter 2

Just as Mr. Moseby left the lobby, London Tipton and her friends Chelsea and Tiffany entered through the revolving door. London's dad owned the hotel so she felt—and acted—like royalty. Dressed in the highest of fashion, as usual, the three girls took stock of the very messy lobby and turned up their noses.

Chelsea looked over at Tiffany. "Tiffany,

are you and your boyfriend coming to my yacht party this weekend?"

"No. My boyfriend, Winthrop *Barrington*, and I are going skiing this weekend." As she spoke, Tiffany put tremendous emphasis on the name Barrington. "We'll be staying at the *Barrington* resort," she went on, "at *Barrington* mountain, in *Barringtonia*." When at last it seemed that Tiffany couldn't find another way to fit in the name Barrington, Chelsea turned to London.

"I would have invited you, but you don't have a boyfriend, and I didn't want you to feel bad." She paused. Then, just in case she hadn't been clear enough, she added, "Because you don't have a boyfriend."

"Actually," London said, tossing her dark hair over her shoulder, "I do have a boyfriend. His name is Lance."

London hoped her voice sounded confident.

She rarely got nervous. Why should she? She was perfect. But telling her friends about Lance was hard. He was *on* her staff—not someone who *had* staff. In her crowd, that was bad news.

At that very moment, Lance Fishman himself walked into the lobby wearing a swimsuit and goggles. "Hey, London!" he called across the lobby. "Check out my new goggles." He smiled, pulling them away from his eyes and then letting them go so they snapped back against his face. He winced. "Okay, that hurt," he said.

London looked on, horrified. Why did Lance have to do that now of all times? Didn't he realize how silly he looked?

"Who's the goofball?" Tiffany asked, mirroring London's thoughts.

The three of them watched Lance massage his eyes. "He's my . . . pool boy," London stammered. Then she checked her watch and said, "Oooh, look at the time!" She grabbed each of her friends by the arm and led them back toward the revolving door. "You two must get going. Thanks for coming! Bye!" she said, hurrying them away so Lance wouldn't catch up to them.

As they disappeared, Lance walked up. "Hey," he said. "How come you never introduce me to your friends? I introduced you to mine."

"Trust me," London said, brushing off the question, "you wouldn't like my friends. I'm not a big fan myself."

It was true—sort of. London knew her friends could be a little stuck up—okay, a lot stuck up. And she didn't really have a lot in common with them other than shopping and fancy parties . . . and shopping. But, they *were* her friends, and there were certain expectations that came with that. One of the biggest of which was that she would not, should not, *could* not, date the hotel staff— even if the guy was a cute lifeguard who was very sweet.

"Something's a little fishy here. And not in a good way," Lance observed. He *really* liked fish. "I think you don't want your friends to meet me."

"Pfft, ta, puh, huh, please," London said, waving her hand in the air. Then she got an idea. "Look, I'll call one of them right now." She grabbed her cell phone and dialed.

On the other end, the phone rang once and someone picked up. "Hey, this is London," she said. "I just want to introduce you to my boyfriend, Lance." Smiling, she pushed the phone into Lance's hand.

"Hi," he said cheerfully. "It's nice to finally meet one of London's friends."

On the other end of the line, Maddie Fitzpatrick smiled. She was the hotel's snack-counter girl but was currently away working as a camp counselor. She knew exactly why Lance was calling from London's phone. The hotel heiress was up to her usual tricks.

"Lance, it's Maddie," she said. "We've met." She was standing in the middle of her cabin, surrounded by her campers.

Lance took the phone away from his ear. "It's Maddie," he repeated, as though London didn't know who she had called. "She doesn't count."

"Hello!" Maddie shouted into her phone. "I can hear you!

"I want to meet your other friends," Lance continued, ignoring Maddie. "The rich, high-society ones that have different noses every time I see them."

For a moment, London just pouted. She hated when her plans didn't work. "Fine," she said. "If it's that important to you, I'll invite them over for tea. But just promise you won't say anything embarrassing like Maddie does."

"Still here!" Maddie said, glaring at her phone. She blew a piece of blond hair out of her eyes. "Did you just call to insult me?" she asked, irritated.

Her question fell on deaf ears. Lance was too happy to care. "Thanks, sweetie," Lance said to London. "You're the best." Then he let out a series of high-pitched squeals. "Eee! Eee! Eee! That's 'I love you' in dolphin," he explained, looking at London admiringly.

"I think that's the sweetest thing I ever heard," London cooed.

Maddie, however, felt differently. "I think I'm going to upchuck on a woodchuck," she said before hanging up. She had campers to deal with and a few minutes on the phone with Lance and London were a few minutes too many.

Chapter 3

Inside the Paul Revere Mini-Mart, Zack was up a very shaky ladder. He was busy doing a rather shoddy job of stacking boxes on a shelf.

Cody walked up and took in the scene. He shook his head disapprovingly. "Sloppy, sloppy, sloppy," he chanted.

"Who cares? Who cares? Who cares?" Zack replied, mocking his brother. Pushing one more box onto the shelf, he started down the ladder. When he was back on solid ground, he began to walk away from his brother.

"Where do you think you're going, mister?" Cody scolded him. "I told you, the labels have to face out! Now go restack that aisle!"

Just then Zack and Cody's mom, Carey, came into the store. The hotel had felt empty without her boys running around, so she had decided to stop by and say hello. "And how are my little minutemen doing?" she asked cheerfully, unaware of the growing tension.

Neither of them acknowledged their mother. "You're not the boss of me!" Zack yelled at Cody.

"Yes, I am!" Cody yelled back.

"Drop dead!" Zack said dismissively.

"You first!" Cody rebutted.

Carey stifled a groan. She had her answer. "That good, huh?" she asked, shaking her head at the twins.

"Look," Cody said to Zack, trying to sound in charge. "Wayne made me the senior bagger. You are the junior trainee bagger, so you *have* to listen to me!"

Zack's blue eyes narrowed. "Do not!" he cried. Then, to prove his point, he covered his ears and started singing at the top of his lungs. "La-la-la-la-la!"

Watching this scene unfold, Carey let out a sigh. It looked as if it was time for some mom advice. "Zack," she began, "if Cody has seniority, then you *do* need to listen to him. And Cody, you can be the boss without being bossy."

"You're bossy," Cody pointed out.

"I'm a mom," she said firmly. "Now, do what I say."

"Please, we don't need lectures at work," Zack said. We get enough of them back at the hotel, he added silently.

"Yeah," Cody agreed. "Just buy your soy kebabs and go home."

As Cody pointed the way—rather rudely it would appear—Wayne walked up. He looked at Carey and then at the twins. "Cody! That is not the Paul Revere way to treat a lady."

"She's no lady," Cody explained. "She's our mom."

Wayne glared at his number one employee.

Stuck between his boss and his mom, Cody sighed. This was not good.

❖❖❖

The next day, London was in the lobby of the Tipton preparing to reveal her goofy boyfriend to her snooty friends.

London had made sure everything was perfect—tea waited to be poured into lovely china, and she had even put out caviar and crackers. Now she sat chatting with Tiffany and Chelsea, awaiting Lance's arrival.

"So, what does your mystery man, Lance, do?" Chelsea asked.

London didn't answer right away. She had to respond to this question very carefully. "He, uh . . . saves lives," she finally said. And he did—sort of. He was a certified lifeguard.

"Oooh!" Tiffany exclaimed. "He's studying to be a doctor?"

Chelsea's eyes widened in delight. "A plastic surgeon?" she asked, giddy at the very notion.

Before London could respond to either of her friends, Lance answered the question for all of them. He walked into the lobby wearing his lifeguard shirt, a swimsuit, and flip-flops. "Hi, sweetie," he said to London. Chelsea and Tiffany looked on, slightly horrified.

London popped out of her seat and pulled Lance aside. "Honey, I told you to wear a suit!" she said.

He looked down at his outfit in confusion. "I am wearing a suit," Lance protested. He didn't see a problem.

"Not a bathing suit!" London cried. "A dress suit. With pockets and other nice stuff!"

"Well, it's got a little pocket on the inside for my keys," Lance explained. "And it's waterproof."

London wanted to crawl under a rock—or find a dressing room to hide in. This meeting was not going well.

"So, London," Chelsea said, slowly putting

two and two together. She had seen Lance yesterday—when London pointed out he was the pool boy. "You're dating your employee. Why?"

Before London could answer, Lance spoke up. "I think she was first attracted to me when I taught her to blow bubbles," he said, picking up a teacup.

London breathed a sigh of relief. Maybe Lance was going to be charming. Maybe he was going to win her friends over the way he had won her over.

But it was not to be. As London watched, Lance brought the cup close to his mouth and began to blow bubbles. Hot tea splattered everywhere!

"Okay, that was hot!" he yelled.

Tiffany giggled. "Well, darling," Tiffany said knowingly, "I can certainly see why you fell for him."

Lance took this as an opening to continue. "Actually, I think I really won her with my whale song," he said, smiling proudly. "It's haunting."

London knew exactly where this was going. Before she could stop him, Lance started to cry out . . . just like a whale! Grabbing a cracker with caviar, she shoved it in his mouth.

"Let's eat!" she suggested.

Lance stopped "singing" to chew. "Hey," he said, his mouth still full, "what is this stuff?"

"Caviar," Tiffany replied, horrified that he didn't know the delicacy. Where on earth had this boy grown up?

"Oh. What's caviar?" Lance asked.

"Fish eggs," Tiffany replied matter-of-factly.

Lance quickly spit out the remnants of the cracker and caviar, much to London's horror.

"Unborn baby fish?! Why don't you just feed me puppies?!" he cried. How could London and her friends be so cruel to poor, defenseless fish?

London had had it. "Lance," she said, gritting her teeth, "a word, dear." When they were out of earshot, London took a deep breath. "You're acting like a goofball!" she hissed.

"I'm just being myself," Lance said.

"Well, don't!" she demanded.

"Then who should I be?" Lance asked, confused.

"Someone who knows the social graces and how to behave in high society!" London shouted. "Otherwise I can't take you to the Gold and Silver Ball." She paused and looked at Lance. "And no, that is not something a seal balances on his nose," she said.

Turning, she nodded to Chelsea and

Tiffany. The girls stood up and together all three strutted out of the lobby. It was time for some much needed retail therapy.

Once London and her girlfriends were gone, Lance was left to contemplate this new development. Things seemed bad. He needed some help. Just then, Arwin walked by, an odd look on his face. "Arwin, do you know how to behave in high society?" Lance asked.

Stopping, Arwin looked over. A pained expression crossed his face. "I can't talk. Must find doctor."

As the man headed toward the door, Lance spotted hundreds of letters on Arwin's back—the corners had snagged his shirt. It didn't look comfortable. Apparently, Arwin hadn't been able to fix his fabulous mail-sorting machine. In fact, it looked as if things had gotten worse.

Lance sighed. His situation wasn't looking much better. He had to figure out how to behave properly. Otherwise, he might lose London.

Chapter 4

Later that afternoon, Zack and Cody were trying—rather unsuccessfully—to work together. As Cody looked on, Zack stacked soup cans into a pyramid. He was doing fine, until, with a loud crash, the structure collapsed.

"That pyramid is pathetic," Cody said with a smirk as his brother began to rebuild the structure. And he would know. He was a superior stacker—Zack could never beat him at this.

Zack looked from his brother to the cans and then back to his brother. An idea was forming in his head—a very good idea indeed. "You're right," Zack said, trying to sound genuine. "I don't know why I even try," he went on dramatically. "Maybe you could show me how to do it, like you did with the apples. 'Bruises in the back!'" he said, quoting his brother enthusiastically. "That was a great tip."

His speech done, Zack stopped and waited to see if his plan—to fool his brother into doing his job—would work. He didn't have to wait long.

"It was, wasn't it?" Cody said, gloating. "Okay, but pay attention," he ordered as he walked over and started restacking Zack's failed pyramid.

Zack took a seat and tried hard to make it look as if he were paying close attention. Inside, he was practically cheering. Cody had fallen for his trap—hook, line . . . and can!

"Labels out. Cans even," Cody was saying as he methodically stacked. "You know, every pyramid starts with a good foundation!"

"You would have made a great Egyptian," Zack said, opening up a big bag of chips and taking out a handful.

"Well, I was thinking about becoming a chiropractor. Get it? Chiro?" Cody said, laughing a little too hard at his own bad joke. Apparently, he thought it was funny because "chiro" sounded like "Cairo," the capital of Egypt.

Zack, of course, thought this was lame, but laughed along anyway. After all, while he was snacking, his brother was doing all the work! "What about the pointy part at the top? Show me how to do that," Zack said, shoveling another handful of chips into his mouth.

Perhaps he had gone too far, or perhaps his mouth had been too full, because Cody stopped what he was doing and looked over at Zack. "Oh, I get it. You're making *me* do all *your* work while you just sit there and eat up the merchandise."

"Okay, okay," Zack said, standing up and handing Cody what was left of the bag. He didn't want to push his luck. Plus, it looked like Cody had taken care of the hard part already.

"Yeah, go finish it," Cody instructed.

Shrugging, Zack picked up the last can and placed it on top gently—just as Wayne walked by.

"Wow, Zack. Great pyramid!" Wayne praised, admiring his work. "You're an amazing stacker!"

"Thanks," Zack said, happily taking the credit.

Turning, Wayne saw Cody standing there, his mouth open, holding the now-empty bag of chips. Reaching out, the manager grabbed the bag out of his hand. "And why are you eating the merchandise?" he asked accusingly.

"I wasn't, Zack was!" Cody cried. He couldn't believe this was happening. Well, actually, he kind of could. But he was not going to let his brother get away with this. "And he didn't stack that! I did! He got me to do it all for him."

Wayne turned back to Zack. "So, you got someone else to do your work for you and then took credit for it?" he pressed.

"Well . . ." Zack started to explain.

"Nice!" Wayne said with a big smile. "You have real management potential." Turning, he walked off toward the produce section.

Zack stood there, beaming. He couldn't believe how well his plan had gone. Getting Cody to do his work for him had been one thing, but Wayne liking his style was a total bonus! He could really get used to this "job" thing.

Turning to Cody, he started to sing, "Wayne likes me better. Wayne likes me better."

"No, he doesn't!" Cody protested.

But at that moment, Wayne came back around the corner from the produce section. Ignoring Cody, he gave Zack a thumbs-up. "Hey, Zack, great job on the apples. Bruises in back." He started to walk away, but not before adding, "I'm promoting Zack to head bagger."

Once he was out of earshot, Zack started his song again. "Second verse, same as the first. Wayne likes me better! Wayne likes me better!"

It was too much. Turning, Cody stormed out of the mini-mart.

Chapter 5

The next day, after another painful morning at work, Cody slumped into the lobby of the Tipton. He couldn't take it anymore. Zack was ruining everything! Cody had had a great gig over at the mini-mart. He had really been *somebody*. Well, he was a bagger—but he had enjoyed the status! And now Zack had taken that away from him! Steam was practically coming out of Cody's ears as he walked across the lobby and ran right smack into Arwin. The man was pushing his failed mail sorter.

"Hey! Watch it!" Arwin said ominously. "This machine will end you! You have *no* idea!"

"It'd probably be for the best," Cody said, sulking. "Zack got a promotion."

"Hey, that's great!" Arwin exclaimed. He sat down to rest.

Cody resisted the urge to roll his eyes. Arwin was a great guy, but sometimes he could be a little . . . oblivious. "No. It's awful," he explained.

"Right! Awful. Awful!" Arwin said. Then he cocked his head. "Why is that awful?"

"Because I used to be Zack's boss, but now he's mine," Cody said, still sulking.

"Good for Zack!" Arwin cheered again,

causing Cody to give him a stern stare. "But very, very bad for you," he added seriously.

"If only there were some way to impress my boss," Cody wondered out loud.

At the word "impress," Arwin's eyes lit up. He had just the thing! "Have you tried touching your tongue to your nose? Wait for it, wait for it . . ." he said, as he inched his tongue out and upward toward his nose, finally reaching it.

Cody quickly tried to get back on topic. Arwin's tongue-to-nose trick was not going to help. He needed something big and brilliant. He would do whatever it took to get back to head bagger. The reality if he didn't was too awful to imagine. "Right now, all Wayne's got me doing is the grunt work, stacking and unstacking shelves," Cody complained.

Once again, Arwin's eyes lit up. He raised

his hand high. "Oooh! Oooh! Oooh! I know this one. Pick me, pick me!"

Cody pointed at Arwin.

"What if," Arwin began, "I could make you the fastest stacker and unstacker in the history of stacking?" He paused. ". . . And, unstacking?"

"You do that," Cody said, his voice rising with excitement, "and you'll never have to pay full price for pretzels ever again."

"Pretzels are my fifth favorite twisty snack treat!" Arwin admitted gleefully as he stood up. Pushing the giant machine, he headed in the direction of his workshop. "Let's go!" he said over his shoulder to Cody.

❖❖❖

As Cody and Arwin headed toward the elevators, Lance came into the lobby seeking some advice. Spotting Mr. Moseby and Carey, he made his way over. Reluctantly, he tapped the manager on the shoulder. "Mr. Moseby," he said, "I really need to talk to you."

Misunderstanding the tap to be one of Lance's usual inane interruptions, the manager turned to him, his expression stern. "For the last time," Mr. Moseby said, "I'm not interested in how long you can hold your breath."

"That's not what it is," Lance pleaded. But now that they were on the subject he thought he might as well tell them. "By the way, three minutes and forty-two seconds." He smiled, but Mr. Moseby was neither amused nor impressed.

Carey, on the other hand, quickly joined Lance in the competition. "I can hold my breath for four minutes and ten seconds," she gloated. The two looked at her curiously.

"Cleaning the boys' bathroom is good practice," she explained with a shrug of her shoulders.

As interesting as this was—and for Lance there wasn't much more exciting than underwater breathing, or nonbreathing—he couldn't be distracted. He needed Mr. Moseby's help. "I just found out that London is embarrassed by me," Lance admitted.

"Nooo!" Mr. Moseby cried, holding a hand to his heart and feigning surprise.

"Yes," Lance said, not picking up on the sarcasm. "She has this Gold and Silver Ball coming up, and I want to go and prove to her that I can fit in with her high-society world. Help me." He looked up at Mr. Moseby with puppy dog eyes.

Mr. Moseby was confused. "Why are you asking me?"

"You're stuck up and snooty," Lance said.

Carey let out a laugh. Lance was right. But if she knew Mr. Moseby, he was going to love, not hate, that description.

And she was right. Mr. Moseby pushed back his shoulders and raised his nose in the air. If for no other reason than to put his essential skills to some good use, he agreed to help Lance.

Chapter 6

Mr. Moseby didn't waste any time. Later that afternoon, Carey sat on her couch and watched Lance nervously pace her apartment. His first lesson in manners was about to commence. Carey hadn't wanted to miss it, so she had happily agreed to let them use her apartment in the hotel. The boys were working, so Lance and Mr. Moseby would have privacy.

"All right," Mr. Moseby started, his tone serious, "I will now teach you proper etiquette and how to comport yourself at a high-society affair."

"Huh?" Lance asked. He sat down next to Carey, already lost.

Carey translated. "He's going to teach you how to talk all fancylike."

Ironically, as she said this, Carey was sitting on the sofa picking at her cuticles—not exactly high-class stuff, Mr. Moseby noted with a sigh. But he had to work with what he had been given. "Correct," Mr. Moseby said. "Now, use your imagination and pretend that Carey is a young, beautiful aristocrat," he said, smiling at his own jab.

"After that you can pretend Moseby's tall enough to see over his desk," Carey shot back.

"Focus, Carey," Mr. Moseby urged. Under his breath he muttered, "Amazon freak."

"But you made me do it," Cody said when Wayne
let Zack out of mini-mart initiation.

"Did you just call to insult me?" Maddie asked
her friend London.

"I think that's the sweetest thing I ever heard,"
London told Lance.

Wayne complimented Zack on his stacking skills.
"Thanks. It's what I do," Zack said.

"Now, pretend that Carey is a young, beautiful
aristocrat," Mr. Moseby said.

"Gentle enough to handle ripe tomatoes, and
it has amazing dexterity," Cody said proudly.

"You don't get out much, do you Mr. Moseby?" Carey asked as they watched Lance and London dance.

"Sweetie, you don't have to change for me," London cooed. "Although I do love that suit."

Carey was a performer so she knew what to do. To get into character, she stuck her nose in the air and held her jaw firm. "So, Lawnce," Carey began, her vowels drawn out.

Lance started to laugh.

"What is so funny?" Mr. Moseby asked, unamused.

"She called me 'Lawnce,'" Lance said, practically snorting with laughter. "Does that mean in the morning, I put on my 'pawnts?'"

"Only if you live in Frawnce," Carey chimed in, beginning to laugh, too.

"You know what?" Mr. Moseby said, clearly exasperated. "If you two aren't going to take this seriously I have more important things to do."

Lance quickly stood up. Mr. Moseby couldn't leave! He needed the manager's help, and he'd do whatever it took. "Come on, Mr. Moseby," he pleaded. Then, before he could stop himself, he added, "Give me one more chawnce." Once again, he broke down into hysterical laughter.

Carey joined in with another giggle until Mr. Moseby glared at her. She cleared her throat and got serious. "Okay, okay. So, Lawnce, tell me, what are your goals in life?" she asked.

"Oh, that's easy," Lance replied. "I want to grow a dorsal fin and gills."

Mr. Moseby wanted to scream. But that would not be very dignified. So instead, he took a deep breath. "Okay, goals that don't involve you becoming a comic-book character," he said. "Let's move on to the culinary arts."

"Huh?" Lance asked, confused once again by the big words.

"Food," Carey translated . . . again.

Mr. Moseby nodded and ushered them to the practice dinner table he had set. "Now, it's important you be familiar with the menu," Mr. Moseby began. "They're serving pâté de foie gras, followed by escargots, and coq au vin in a Roquefort reduction."

Lance looked at Mr. Moseby as though he'd grown a second head and was speaking in a foreign language. He turned to Carey for yet another explanation.

"Liver, snails, and chicken with mold," Carey said.

Lance nodded. "I'll eat before I go," he said.

"Good idea," Carey agreed.

Again, Mr. Moseby decided it was safer to simply move on then try to demonstrate the importance of culinary masterpieces. "Let's talk about wardrobe. Did you bring a suit?"

Lance nodded. He headed over to where he had hung his suit and grabbed the jacket. "I don't own any nonbathing suits, so I borrowed my brother's," he said as Mr. Moseby and Carey watched.

Lance pulled on the enormous coat—he could easily have fit three of him in it. "He's a fat man . . ." Lance started to explain. Before he could go on, the lapels of the suit lit up with flashy bulbs. ". . . in a circus," he finished with a smile.

Mr. Moseby stood there, speechless. He would need to pull out all the stops if he was going to have any hope of turning Lance into London's Prince Charming.

❖❖❖

While Lance was busy training for his big night with London, she was busy panicking about it. There was only one person who could help her with this mess she'd gotten herself into. She pulled out her cell phone and dialed.

Stuck at camp, Maddie had never been so glad to hear her cell phone ring—civilization calling!

The camp-counselor job wasn't going exactly as she had hoped, and though she hated to admit it, she was a little lonely. When she picked up, London's voice was cheerful on the other end. "Hey Maddie!" she said. "It's London! So, how's camp going?"

"Oh, swell," Maddie said sarcastically. Her hair was an unkempt mess, and her clothes were practically torn to threads. "Last night somebody thought it would be cute to put a wolverine in my sleeping bag." As she said this, she glanced over at her innocent-looking little campers. *Not so innocent*, thought Maddie.

But London, as usual, didn't have time for Maddie's insignificant problems. Her voice turned serious. "Glad you're having fun," she said, completely ignoring the mention of a wolverine. "On to me," she continued. "I have to break up with Lance."

Maddie was confused. "I thought you liked him," she said.

"I do," London admitted, "but he doesn't fit in with my friends."

"London, how can you expect your friends to accept Lance the way he is, if you won't?" Maddie asked.

"Well, what should I do?" London asked, pouting.

"Instead of trying to change him, why don't *you* try to change a little?" Maddie suggested.

London thought about this for a minute. Could the solution be that simple? No! "I am not growing gills. At least until they invent diamond gill rings," she said.

Maddie stifled the urge to groan. Getting through to London was never easy. "Why don't you start with human organs, like a heart or a brain? Gotta go," she said and hung up the phone. She had her own set of problems to deal with.

One of her campers, Holly, looked over at her. "So, what's going on with London?" she asked. Living in the same cabin, they knew all about the Tipton, the twins, London, Lance, and the various dramas.

"Boyfriend problems," Maddie explained to Holly, Jasmine, Amy, and Leah. "But you guys are too young to hear about that sort of stuff."

"I have a boyfriend," Holly pointed out.

"I've had two," Jasmine chimed in.

"I've had three," said Leah.

Then Amy had the last word. "I'm married," she said. They all stared at her. "We're separated," she shrugged.

Maddie raised her eyebrows. She *had* to find a way out of this place. . . .

Chapter 7

The night of the Gold and Silver ball arrived. While Lance and London had their own problems to deal with, Cody was busy with his. This was his last chance to get his job back in order.

Inside the mini-mart, Wayne and Zack were unaware of Cody's plan. Wayne was ringing up a cute girl's groceries while Zack bagged them. "You know," Wayne said, trying to sound suave, "we're having a special. Buy one, get *Wayne* free." He chuckled at his own lame pick-up line.

The girl was not impressed. In fact, she was appalled at this suggestion. As soon as she paid, she quickly ran out of the store. Zack looked at Wayne. "The only things sharper than that line are your finely chiseled features," Zack said earnestly.

"You kissing up to the boss?" Wayne asked.

"Yes," Zack replied. He had no problem admitting this. He knew that kissing up to Wayne meant better treatment and a better title. If that's what it took to stay ahead of Cody, he had no problem playing Wayne's game.

"Well done," Wayne said. "Where's your brother?"

As if on cue, a pulsing beat filled the store. A moment later, Cody appeared from the back aisle, wearing a metallic contraption that consisted of four arms complete with extensions, pinchers, and suction cups. He began to make his way toward the checkout counter. Arwin followed close behind.

"It's the alien invasion! Take the boy!" Wayne cried, thrusting Zack in front of Cody.

But Zack knew what was going on. "It's not an alien invasion. It's a dork invasion," he explained. Looking at his brother's odd costume, he rolled his eyes. "What are you doing?" he asked Cody.

"Showing Wayne which one of us really deserves to be senior bagger," Cody replied. "This baby will improve stacking efficiency by fifty percent."

"Actually it's fifty-five percent," Arwin whispered, trying not to be noticed. But his whisper was loud. Wayne and Zack looked at him, waiting for further explanation. He didn't offer much. "Just something I threw together from an old letter sorter I had lying around." Then, distracted by the candy display, he walked away to get a closer—and hopefully, tastier—look.

Cody shrugged. He was too eager to show off his high-efficiency bag-boy accessory to wait for Arwin. "Check this out," he said, turning the suit on. He moved to a big box filled with cans and started to stack them on the shelf, double-timing it with his double arms. "See? It stacks twice as much," he said, looking at Wayne for approval.

Wayne was definitely impressed. Any way he could get more done by doing less was always appealing to him. "Excellent," he said, nodding.

"You haven't seen anything yet," Cody added. All four arms of the machine started to turn cans around on the shelves. "See? It turns labels out, too." One arm stopped to wipe Cody's brow, even as the other three arms kept working. "Oooh, thanks," Cody said.

He moved on to the produce section and picked up some tomatoes. "Gentle enough to handle ripe tomatoes, and it has amazing dexterity," Cody explained. He was starting to sound like an infomercial!

The machine began to juggle the tomatoes. Both Wayne and Zack were clearly impressed. This was quite a display, indeed! "This is only half speed. Watch this!" Cody said, flipping the double-time switch. But the switch broke off. "Uh-oh," Cody said, "that can't be good."

Suddenly, the machine arms started to flail around like crazy, picking up tomatoes and tossing them all over the place. When there were no more tomatoes, the arms grabbed a box of crackers and began to throw them at Zack.

"Cody, quit it!" Zack ordered.

"It's not me! I don't know what's wrong with this thing!" Cody yelled over the noise of the machine. As if to prove Cody's point, the machine slapped him.

"Get back! Get back!" Wayne yelled.

Not one to back down from a challenge, Zack grabbed a salami. "That's how you want it?!" Zack asked. "Bring it on!" He began batting away at the flying crackers.

Unbothered, the machine's arm went after Wayne. It grabbed hold of him and pinched. "Ahhhh! It's getting fresh with me!"

Arwin looked on in horror. It was the mail-sorting incident all over again! "Hit the red button!" he yelled.

Cody frantically looked all over the

machine. "There is no red button!"

"I always forget the red button," Arwin lamented.

"I'll save you, Wayne!" Zack yelled, diving toward the machine.

"Arwin," Cody pleaded, "stop this crazy thing!"

"Okay, I'm goin' in!" Arwin said, as he ducked under everyone and reached around to the back of the machine. With one quick pull, he removed the battery. And then, with one last electronic gasp, the machine arms went limp.

All that was left now was the biggest mess the Paul Revere Mini-Mart had ever seen. And it was all Cody's fault.

"Cody," Wayne said to him. "I've got a better way to improve the store. You're fired!"

At the ball, Lance's big night was about to begin. It *had* to go well. If it didn't, it wouldn't be because he hadn't tried.

Tiffany, Chelsea, and their boyfriends, Tyler and Winthrop, were milling around, making small talk about who was wearing what and who looked great and who looked terrible, when the discussion turned to Lance. "Wait until you meet London's boyfriend. He is such a goof." Tiffany laughed.

As if on cue, Lance entered the room. His hair was slicked back, his tux fit like a glove, and he looked like a million bucks. A million *gorgeous* bucks. Chelsea and Tiffany were stunned.

Lance headed toward them. "Good evening, ladies," he said with a smile. "Gentlemen." He shook each boy's hand firmly. "It's Fishman, Lance Fishman," he said in true James Bond style. "It's so lovely to be at the dance."

Chelsea moved in toward him. "Wow, Lance. You clean up good." She swooned.

Lance shook his head at this. "I believe it's, 'well,'" he corrected her.

Carey and Mr. Moseby had snuck in to watch the big event and were lurking in the doorway, taking in the whole scene. They couldn't believe their eyes. "By George, I think he's got it," Carey said, shocked at the transformation.

"George had nothing to do with it," Mr. Moseby said. "It was all me."

Meanwhile, Lance was getting impatient to see London. After all, she was the reason he had gone through all this. He didn't care about impressing everyone else in the room. He was only there to make one person proud. "Perchance, have you seen London?

I got a message she'd meet me here," he said to the girls, staying in character.

Tiffany looped her arm through Lance's. "Who needs her?" she said slyly. "Winthrop, go to the bathroom," she directed her boyfriend.

"Tyler, go with him," Chelsea said, looping her arm through Lance's free arm. Tyler and Winthrop gave them both looks of annoyance. But, they trudged away toward the bathroom as they'd been told.

Just then, London made her grand entrance—or rather, her spashtacular entrance. Instead of a ball gown and jewels, she was wearing a surfing outfit, complete with board shorts, a tank top, and flip-flops. She even had floaties around her arms!

Chelsea was scandalized. "Oh, my—"

"London?!" Tiffany cried, equally appalled.

"Hi, guys," London said cheerfully.

"Have you seen Lance?" She had no idea she was looking right at her boyfriend.

"I'm right here," Lance said.

London's jaw almost hit the floor. This was Lance? *Her* Lance? "Wow, you look like a million bucks," she said.

Chelsea was not to be distracted. "What are you wearing that for?" she asked with a certain amount of disgust in her voice.

"It's a black-tie event, honey," Lance reminded her. He turned to Chelsea and Tiffany and tried to explain. "She must have just come from her yacht," he suggested, thinking he was covering for London.

"No, I dressed this way on purpose," London protested.

"Oh, London. How droll of you," Lance said.

London squinted her eyes suspiciously. "Who are you, and what have you done with my boyfriend?" she asked.

"I made him someone you could be proud of," Lance said.

"You didn't have to do all of that. I dressed this way so you wouldn't feel out of place with my obnoxious, snobby friends." She looked at her friends apologetically. "No offense, girls.

"None taken," Chelsea said.

"You pegged it," Tiffany agreed.

The haughty expression on Lance's face disappeared as he broke into a huge grin. "You are the sweetest." Lance said, glowing.

"No, *you're* the sweetest." London beamed.

Lance grabbed a rose and handed it to London. She accepted it graciously, and the two of them moved toward the dance floor.

From their spot in the doorway, Mr. Moseby and Carey enjoyed the outcome of their handiwork, although Mr. Moseby was enjoying it more than Carey.

"It's just so romantic," he said, choking back tears.

Carey looked over at him. "You don't get out much, do you Mr. Moseby?"

On the dance floor, London and Lance smiled at one another. "Sweetie," London said, "you don't have to change for me. Although I do love that suit."

"And I love those flip-flops," Lance said.

"I love your cuff links," London replied.

"And I love your floaties," Lance said. Only London could make floaties work as a fashion accessory.

The music began to play, and Lance and London started to slow dance. Chelsea and Tiffany looked on. "They look so happy together," Tiffany observed. "I think I want to date one of my employees."

Chelsea gave this some thought and

agreed. "I think I'll date my chauffeur. I wonder what the front of his head looks like."

Shrugging, they went to look for their boyfriends while Lance and London danced the night away, he in his tux and she in her swimsuit.

Chapter 8

Back at the mini-mart, the scene was more messy than glitzy. Zack was trying to clean up his brother's mess while Arwin was trying to salvage some part of his mail-sorter-turned-tomato-thrower.

Cody approached Zack. His folded apron and hat were in hand. "Well, Zack, you're the head bagger," he said, handing his brother the uniform. "Although, without me there is no head bagger. Ironic, huh?" he asked.

"I'll tell you what's ironic," Zack said, getting revved up about the whole situation. This work thing had taken a bad turn. "You get fired and I have to clean up your mess."

Arwin walked over to them. He was wearing the superstacking machine. "Well, maybe this will teach you guys not to be so competitive. Boy, did you two screw up," he said. The boys gave him a look. How were they supposed to take advice from a guy wearing a malfunctioning robot suit. Arwin noted the looks on their faces. "Of course," he said, self-consciously, "that's just one four-armed man's opinion."

Cody nodded. Arwin did have a point. He had messed up, and Wayne had fired him. There was nothing left to do. It was time to go. "Well, see ya," he said to Zack. Turning, his shoulders slumped in defeat, he started to walk away.

Zack felt a rush of guilt. If he thought about it for a minute, a lot of this was his fault. Well, more like a *little* of it was his fault. Most of it was his dorky brother's fault.

Nevertheless, it had been Cody who got Zack the job, and it had been Zack's laziness that drove Cody into Arwin's robot arms. And it had been those arms that got Cody fired. . . . Zack realized he'd better do something.

"Hey, wait a minute," he said to Cody. His brother paused at the entrance hopefully. "Wayne," Zack said, walking over to his boss. "Look, I know Cody messed up, and he's annoying, and he micromanages, and he snores. . . ." He paused for a minute wondering where he was going with this. "I lost my point. . . ."

"Cody . . . messing up . . ." Wayne reminded him.

"Oh, yeah!" Zack said. "Give him another chance."

Cody turned fully. Was his brother really going to bat for him?

But then Zack continued. "We need worker bees around here. You're not going to find another gem like him," he said to Wayne.

Cody groaned. Not exactly what he'd wanted to hear.

Wayne thought about this. It was true. They could always use a worker bee. Maybe Zack was right. Maybe he had been too hasty. "You're right. Cody, I'm hiring you back."

"You are?" Cody asked.

Wayne nodded. "You're the head bag boy, again," he added.

Zack hadn't expected this. "What?!" he yelled.

"No, no," Cody protested. True, it would be nice to have the title back. But he'd learned his lesson. "That's what got us in trouble. We should be equals."

"You mean equal with each other, right? 'Cause to me, you're both just my helper monkeys," Wayne explained.

"Understood," Zack nodded.

"Fine by me," Cody agreed, smiling.

Arwin was probably happiest of all—after all, it was his invention that had caused all the trouble in the first place. "Give me a high twenty!" he said to Zack and Cody, holding up all of his hands.

So maybe the transition to working together hadn't exactly gone smoothly, but at least the worst was over. Now Zack and Cody just had to figure out a way to get rid of that silly stacking machine once and for all! From here on out they were doing the stacking the old-fashioned way!

Get More of Your Favorite Pop Star!

HANNAH MONTANA

Includes 8 full-color postcards!

Poster Book

From the hit TV series on Disney Channel

Bonus:
8 postcards to
send to friends!

Includes 12 posters of the show's stars!

**Collect all the stories
about Hannah Montana!**

Don't Bet on It

Sweet Revenge

Win or Lose

DISNEY PRESS

**Available wherever
books are sold**

www.disneybooks.com